Other advent

Bait for a Burglar

Bait for a Burglar

By Joan Lowery Nixon

Disney PRESS

114 Fifth Avenue
New York, NY 10011-5690

For Eileen and Katie J.
with love.—J. L. N.

First Disney Press paperback 1997
Text © 1997 by Joan Lowery Nixon.

Printed in the United States of America.

1 3 5 7 9 10 8 6 4 2

Library of Congress Catalog Card Number: 96-72038
ISBN: 0-7868-4089-7 (pbk.)

Bait for a Burglar

1

BRIAN QUINN TOOK a deep breath and tried to keep his mind on what he was doing. He looked at the other eighth-grade students in his class, then back to the paper he was clutching. It was hard enough to have to read what he'd written to the rest of the class, but what Dad had said this morning bothered him. He couldn't concentrate.

"There's a high-tech burglar loose in Redoaks. We need to upgrade our insurance policy," Mr. Quinn had said in an undertone to his wife, but Brian had overheard.

"What high-tech burglar? Where is he? What are you talking about, Dad?" Brian had asked.

Mr. Quinn had looked at his watch. "Better hurry, Brian, or you'll be late for school. I'll tell you about it this evening."

Ms. McGowan, who taught journalism, broke into Brian's thoughts. "Well, Brian?" she asked. "Are you ready?"

Brian gulped and nodded. "Death is never good to talk about," he read somberly. "But yesterday, in Mr. Hightower's eleven o'clock biology class, death was on every student's mind. Maybe they didn't learn how to dissect frogs—which was the lesson of the day. But they learned lessons in life and death and in standing up for one's beliefs. Four students, who called the frog a creature to be respected, refused to take part in the lesson."

Brian added the details of the news story, then said, "The end." He gave such a loud sigh of relief, his friends laughed.

Brian laughed, too. He had thought journalism would be an easy A, but every time he had to stand in front of the class and read a news story he'd written, he groaned inside. The kids in the class gave a lot of grief to anyone who made even the slightest mistake. Ms. McGowan was tough, too.

Up went a hand. Amanda asked, "Brian, what kind of research did you do? Are you sure they were frogs and not toads?"

Brian reddened, but he said, "Mr. Hightower told us they were frogs. He's the teacher. He'd know."

"How about Mr. Hightower? Did you check him out? Does he have the proper background to teach biology?"

Ms. McGowan took charge. "Thank you, Amanda, but the research you're suggesting isn't important to the story. It's not about Mr. Hightower's background or even the frogs. The point of the story is that four students stood up for something in which they believed."

"Good job," she said to Brian, "although . . ." She smiled at him as though they shared a good joke, then went on. "Your story was interesting and informative, but just a little too dramatic."

As Brian walked to his seat, Ms. McGowan told the class, "Many reporters tend to get emotional about their stories. It's a habit that's easy to fall into. But I want to break you of it now. That's my job. *Your* job is to give people information, not opinions. Let your readers or viewers become outraged or sympathetic by your *facts,* not by your adjectives and adverbs."

Brian's best friend, Sam, reached across the aisle to punch Brian on the arm. "You looked so cool," Sam whispered. "I have to read my story tomorrow, and I already feel like barfing."

Brian tuned Sam out. Ms. McGowan had called Estella Martinez's name.

Estella faced the class and said, "My news story has to do with food waste in the school cafeteria." She began to read, and Brian was impressed with her investigation. Estella hadn't just interviewed just the cafeteria manager, she'd also interviewed Miss Alice, one of the lunch line attendants, and Mr. Maxx, the custodian. All three gave their opinions about how much food was actually being thrown away.

When Estella finished, a few of her friends applauded and Estella blushed.

"I know she's pretty, but stop staring," Sam whispered to Brian.

"Get lost," Brian mumbled.

Ms. McGowan beamed at Estella. "That was an excellent reporting job," she said. "You gave us all the facts, and your interviews were wonderful. What a good idea to get Mr. Maxx's opinion. Great work!"

The bell rang, and—as usual—there was a great deal of noise as all the kids picked up their books and got ready for the next class.

"Sam, Cindy, Danny, and Marion," Ms. McGowan called out. "You'll read your news stories tomorrow. Brian and Estella, I need to see you both for a moment, please."

What did I do now? Brian wondered as he walked to Ms. McGowan's desk. He glanced at Estella, who whispered, "What's this all about, Brian?"

Brian took a deep breath. "We'll soon find out," he said.

2

Ms. McGowan pulled two pieces of paper from a folder. She handed one to Brian and one to Estella. Brian took a quick glance and saw that it was a printed form.

"You two have a real talent for journalism. That's why I immediately thought of you for Channel Two's program, *That's News 2 Me*," she said and smiled.

Estella stood up straighter, her brown eyes huge. "Do you mean that local television news show for kids on Saturday mornings?"

"That's right," Ms. McGowan answered.

"The producer has invited all the schools in the greater Redoaks area to take part. The kids who are picked will have a week to work behind the scenes as editors, camera people, and reporters. I was told to choose two reporters."

Brian tried to take it all in. Ms. McGowan wanted him to be a reporter on TV? He didn't think he'd like that at all. He *did* like being a Casebuster with his nine-year-old brother Sean. The Casebusters' private investigations were done quietly—even secretly.

On television, anything he investigated would be in front of the cameras with everybody in Redoaks watching! Brian gulped. It was scary just to stand up and read a news story in front of his journalism class. Think what it would be like to know that hundreds—no, thousands—of people were watching!

There was no way he was going to put himself in that spot. But he couldn't say so because Ms. McGowan was still talking. Brian tried to pay attention.

"You'll be given story ideas from the assignments editor," she said. "Then you'll do the research, the interviews, you'll write the report, and give it on the air." She smiled. "What do you think?"

While Brian tried to come up with a polite way to say "no," Estella bounced a few times, hugged her books to her chest, and said, "Oh, yes! I'll do it!" She glanced at Brian and grinned. "You will, too, won't you, Brian? We can work together."

All of Brian's doubts immediately vanished. Instead of saying "no," he found himself saying, "Sure. I'll do it, too, Ms. McGowan."

"That's great," Ms. McGowan said. "Have

your parents sign the permission slips I gave you. On Monday afternoon you'll meet with the Channel Two assignments editor and the other students who are working on this project. And please remember, I'm here if you need me."

"Thank you, Ms. McGowan," Estella said.

"Uh—yeah, thanks," Brian added.

"Congratulations and good luck," Ms. McGowan said.

As they left the classroom Estella clasped Brian's hand. Her eyes shone as she said, "This is going to be great. I can't wait to tell my mom. It's going to be so much fun working with you, Brian. You really did a great job with your news story."

Brian's mouth opened, but his heart started thumping. All he could manage to say was, "Uh, thanks. Right now I guess we gotta go to class."

*　　*　　*

Brian felt as if he were in the shower while the dishwasher was running and the water went from hot to cold and back again. One minute he was happy with the idea of working with Estella. The next minute he'd think about having to give a report to all those eyes watching their TV sets.

Brian kept his news until his family was seated around the dinner table that night. "Guess what," he said. "I'm going to be on TV."

"When?" Mrs. Quinn asked.

"Where?" Mr. Quinn said.

"How come?" Sean asked, his mouth filled with mashed potatoes.

"Ms. McGowan picked Estella Martinez and me to represent Redoaks Junior High on *That's News 2 Me*," Brian said. "We'll be investigative reporters."

"Wow!" Sean shouted. "You'll be a television star!"

"No. I'll just be on TV once," Brian explained. "And then it's another school's turn. Estella and I have to get our stories ready in a week. Then on Thursday we'll be filmed, the tape will be edited on Friday, and the show will air on Saturday morning."

"Cool," Sean said. He shoved another forkful of mashed potatoes into his mouth.

"We're proud of you, Brian," Mr. Quinn said.

Mrs. Quinn's eyes sparkled. "We'll tell all of our friends," she said. "Everyone will be watching."

Everyone will be watching? Brian shuddered. It will be great working with Estella, he thought, but will it really be worth it?

The Quinns ate in silence for a few

moments. Then Brian said, "Dad, what about the High-Tech Burglar?"

"What's a high-tech burglar?" Sean asked.

"He's not someone to be afraid of," Mr. Quinn cautioned. "He's someone to be prepared for." He turned to Mrs. Quinn. "After dinner let's talk about taking out a special insurance policy on our computers, printer, fax . . . all our electronic equipment."

"Doesn't our homeowners policy offer them?" Mrs. Quinn asked.

"Only to a point," he said. "It doesn't offer complete coverage, and under the circumstances . . ."

"Why are you worried about our computers and stuff? What's going on, Dad?" Brian asked.

"The police have seen a tremendous rise in home burglaries in Redoaks within the last month," Mr. Quinn answered.

"I haven't read anything about it in the newspaper," Mrs. Quinn said.

"The police have been keeping the burglaries quiet, and the reporter on the police beat hasn't picked up on the news yet," Mr. Quinn said.

"Why are they keeping the burglaries quiet?" Sean asked.

"Because they're not your usual burglaries," Mr. Quinn explained. "The police feel that the burglaries are being committed by one person. And what makes them unusual is that only electronic equipment is being taken."

"Like computers," Sean said.

"Yes, computers, VCRs, fax machines, electronic games, TV cameras, and other electronic equipment—all of which can easily be sold and not traced. The police have nicknamed the thief the High-Tech Burglar."

"Have they found any of the stolen stuff in pawnshops or other places where it might be sold?" Brian asked.

"No, and that's another strange thing about these burglaries," Mr. Quinn said. "None of the stolen items have shown up in or around Redoaks."

"Weird," Sean said.

Mr. Quinn went on. "Also, the crook isn't just targeting wealthy people. He's also stealing from apartments and middle-class homes, such as ours."

"So he knows who owns electronic equipment," Brian said. "Are you investigating this case, Dad?"

"No," Mr. Quinn said. "It's being handled by the police."

And maybe, Brian thought, by the Casebusters. He raised his eyebrows in a question as he looked at Sean. In answer, Sean nodded. Satisfied, Brian knew they were in agreement. The case might be too tough for the police to solve, but he'd like the Casebusters to give it a try.

Kids make good private investigators, because grown-ups hardly ever pay attention to kids. Of course, sometimes Brian and Sean were in danger, and then things got kind of hairy.

Brian shook his head and went back to eating his dinner. He wasn't going to worry about the bad times now!

Mrs. Quinn let out a sigh. "I'd hate to lose our camcorder and any family photos still in it. It's bad enough to be burglarized," she said, "but the thieves steal memories as well as the camera." She smiled at Brian and Sean. "Someday, I'd like to pass on all those wonderful growing-up photos to your wives."

"Wives? Gross!" Sean made a face and clutched his stomach. "You can't give anything to my wife, because I'm never getting married."

"I bet you will," Brian teased. He made kissing noises. "I bet you'll grow up and marry Debbie Jean Parker."

"Yuck! Quit it! Mom!" Sean yelled. He tried to shove Brian out of his chair.

"That's enough," Mrs. Quinn said firmly.

But Sean smirked at Brian. "How about you and Estella Martinez?" He began to sing, "Two little lovebirds sitting in a tree. K-i-s-s-i-n-g."

Brian felt his face grow hot. "Where'd you learn a dumb song like that?" he asked.

Sean grinned. "From Grandma. She told me I'd know when to use it."

"Quiet down, boys," Mr. Quinn said. He

turned to Mrs. Quinn. "Just for safety's sake, I'll insure our electronic equipment. Agreed?"

"Dad, let me ask you a question," Brian said. "What makes you think the High-Tech Burglar is going to hit us?"

"Let me ask you a question," Mr. Quinn said. "What makes you think he won't?"

3

ON SATURDAY morning Mrs. Quinn drove Brian and Estella to the Channel Two station. She told them what time she'd pick them up.

"Thanks, Mrs. Quinn," Estella said, as she climbed from the car. "My mom thanks you, too. She couldn't leave work. Saturday's one of her busiest days."

Mrs. Quinn smiled. "No problem, Estella. I'm glad you can ride with us."

As Mrs. Quinn drove off, Estella took a brush from her purse and smoothed down her hair. "Your mom's really nice," Estella said.

She smiled at Brian. "Do I look okay?"

"Okay? Estella, you look really . . . uh . . ." Brian gulped. "Yeah, really okay."

Brian and Estella walked into the television station through the main doors and stood in front of the receptionist's desk.

"May I help you?" the receptionist asked.

"We're here for—" Brian began.

A telephone rang, and the receptionist said, "Channel Two . . . The panel is on at nine o'clock tonight."

She looked up, and Brian said, "This is Estella Martinez and I'm—"

"Channel Two," the receptionist said into the phone as it rang again. "Please hold, and I'll connect you with the program manager."

She looked up again, and Brian spoke as fast as he could. "And I'm Brian Quinn. We're here for *That's News 2 Me.*"

The phone rang yet again. The receptionist said, "Channel Two. Hold please." To Brian she said, "Third door on the left." Into the phone she said, "Channel Two. Yes, Jack. Sales meeting Wednesday. . . . Channel Two . . ."

"C'mon," Brian said to Estella. "Third door on the left."

As they walked down a long, quiet hallway, Estella stopped smiling and began to look a little scared. Suddenly, she stopped. "Here's the third door," she said.

Brian's hand was clammy on the doorknob, but he managed to open the door and step inside, following Estella.

The room they entered was painted black, and banks of stage lights were on, making it incredibly bright. Brian and Estella blinked for a few seconds, letting their eyes adjust to the light.

"Hey, Quinn," someone called. Brian looked around the room and saw faces that were familiar because he'd seen them on *That's News 2 Me,* and a couple more he thought he recognized from Redoaks Junior High. But it took Brian a moment to recognize the guy in the blue shirt and jeans who had spoken to him and was now smiling.

"Hi, Jack," Brian said. He put his hand on Estella's shoulder and led her to meet Jack Bowman.

Jack had been a ninth-grader in Redoaks Junior High when Brian was in seventh grade. They were both on the student council and worked together on the Book Fair committee. Brian liked Jack, and he felt bad that some of the kids avoided Jack after hearing he'd been arrested for shoplifting. According to the rumors Brian had heard, Jack's parents took him back to the store to return what he'd taken, but the store pressed charges anyway. That was over a year ago. For all Brian knew, Jack might still be on probation.

"This is cool," Brian said as he glanced around the studio. "What kind of job do you have here?"

Jack ran his hand through his blond hair. "I work on *That's News 2 Me* every week as a cameraman."

"That's great."

A tall redheaded girl, who was seated nearby, leaned toward Brian and reached out to shake his hand. "Hi," she said. "I'm Holly Knowles, a sound engineer. You can call me a computer and media whiz. My dad likes to joke that not only will I someday be a NASA engineer, but I can even set the programming on our VCR." Holly threw back her head, laughing loudly.

Jack rolled his eyes. "I have to work with her," he whispered to Brian.

Brian recognized Holly from school. She was a bossy, take-charge kind of person. Unfortunately, she also knew what she was doing.

"I'd like you to meet Estella Martinez," Brian said.

"Hi," Estella said.

"Hi," Holly answered. "Glad you're here."

"I'm excited about being here, even if it's just for a week," Estella said.

"It's a lot of fun," Jack agreed.

"How did you get this job?" Estella asked.

"The producers went to the schools in and around Redoaks and asked members of the photography clubs to audition. I did, and so did a guy named Mark from another school. Our teachers recommended us, and we were chosen. Holly and Megan were picked from the media departments, and the four students who work as anchors were chosen from the drama departments at their schools."

Two adults entered the room. One was a scrawny guy with thin, black hair. He was dressed in jeans and a T-shirt and introduced himself as Pete Carter, assignments editor.

The other was a tall, thin woman with bushy brown hair. She told Estella and Brian that she was Sara Jeffries, the producer of *That's News 2 Me*.

"Congratulations on joining our program for the week," she said. "Are you ready to get started?"

Both Brian and Estella nodded, so Sara said, "Okay. Here's the setup. Each of our investigative reporters is teamed with one camera person and one sound engineer. Our entire group will hold a story meeting in which ideas for the show will be pitched.

"Once the ideas are decided on, Pete will give the teams their assignments and make a few suggestions about various angles on the story. I'll help in any way possible. Filming will be completed on Thursday so that the show can be edited on Friday. The reporters will do any extra work that's needed on the stories on Friday, as well."

Pete broke in and said, "When you're being filmed, don't wear white, small plaids, or stripes because they don't read well on camera."

It was Sara's turn. She looked at her notes and said, "Okay, here's how we've teamed you. Team one: Estella, Megan, and Jack. Team two: Brian, Mark, and Holly."

Brian glanced at Estella with a pang of disappointment.

Jack whispered, "Tough break, Brian."

Sara called out to the other kids in the room, "Story meeting. Everybody over here."

Chairs were dragged and rearranged into a circle, until all the people who helped make *That's News 2 Me* were included.

"Now," Sara said, "let's hear some ideas."

For a few moments there was only silence. Then Estella shyly raised her hand, an inch at a time, until it was barely over her head.

Brian knew how Estella felt. It was like school, when you sort of know the answer, but you're not sure, so you don't want anyone to laugh if you're wrong.

"Estella, you're not in a classroom," Sara said bluntly. "You don't need to raise your hand. Just speak out."

Estella's voice was tiny. "Uh . . . I'd like to do a story about the way the news is produced."

Sara closed her eyes and rubbed her chin as she thought. "A behind-the-scenes sort of thing?" She turned to Pete. "What are your ideas on this?"

"I like the idea of behind-the-scenes," Pete said, "but not on us. How about investigating people who have unusual occupations?"

Sara began to seem interested. "Like a medical photographer? Or a—"

"A professional pet sitter?" Estella said.

"Yeah. Good. That's the idea," Pete said.

"A stage set painter," one of the anchors suggested.

"A hot-air-balloon pilot," Holly screeched.

"A seal trainer," Megan giggled.

Soon everyone had contributed ideas, and the list of unusual jobs grew. Estella's cheeks were pink with excitement.

Finally Sara said, "Okay. The members of

the first team have a good start on their topic." She turned to Brian and asked, "What have you come up with, Brian?"

Everyone stared at Brian as he blurted out, "I'd like to do a story about the high-tech burglaries."

Sara quickly shook her head. "Forget that idea right now," she said. "That news story is not for us."

4

BRIAN DIDN'T give up easily. "Why not?" he asked. "I think it's a good idea."

Sara glanced at Pete before she said, "For one thing, the police have asked us not to make a big thing of the burglaries. If they're kept low-key the police think they'll have a better chance of catching the thief."

"And for another thing," Pete interrupted, "burglaries are too much for a news show for kids. Besides, the nightly news team is already working on that story. When it breaks it won't be on *That's News 2 Me*."

"So come up with something else," Sara

said. "C'mon, Brian, give us another idea."

For a panicky moment Brian went blank, but Estella spoke up. "Kids *do* think about burglaries and robberies. So how about safety tips? You know, like not opening doors to strangers, writing down license plate numbers of suspicious cars, when to call 9-1-1 emergency, and when to call the regular phone number of the police. That sort of thing."

Sara perked up. "It not only gives good information. It also teaches commonsense prevention. I like it. Pete? Your opinion, please."

Pete stared into space for a moment, then said, "Yeah. It'll work. Go for it, Brian. Have the first draft of your script ready for us on Monday."

As Estella smiled at Brian he no longer minded that his story idea had been changed so much. Crime prevention would be interesting, too.

*   *   *

When Mrs. Quinn picked up Brian and Estella after the meeting, they were both excited about their projects.

"We even found a way to link our stories," Estella said. "Sara suggested that I do three short interviews. The third could be an interview with a police sketch artist or fingerprint expert. That could lead right into Brian's story about crime prevention."

"You're both doing a terrific job," Mrs. Quinn said. "I have an idea, too, if you'd like to hear it."

"Sure, Mom," Brian said.

"It's really for Estella and not you, Brian," Mrs. Quinn answered. "I was thinking about your mother's job, Estella. It's a very interesting one. Maybe you could interview her."

"I doubt it. Mom's kind of shy," Estella said. But she smiled as she added, "I'll ask her."

Mrs. Quinn drove up in front of the apartment Estella shared with her mother.

As Estella climbed out of the car, Brian said, "I'll see you tomorrow, Estella, when the teams get together."

Estella said, "Our news stories will have to be outlined by then. Tomorrow! We've got an awful lot of research and writing to do."

Brian climbed into the front seat as his mother drove toward home. He asked, "What kind of job does Mrs. Martinez have? Why is it so interesting?"

"Mrs. Martinez owns a travel agency," Mrs. Quinn answered.

"She's a travel agent?" Brian groaned. "Aw, Mom, kids want to learn about cool jobs like sewer inspectors, or night watchmen in cemeteries, or the guys who feed blood to bats in the zoo."

"There are lots of people who might think that planning people's travel is interesting," Mrs. Quinn said, but Brian just shook his head. He was glad that Estella had said her mother was shy and would turn down the idea.

*   *   *

That evening, as all the Quinns pitched in to get dinner ready, Sean said, "When I rode down to the park, I ran into Jacob Dean, one of the kids in my class, and he said—"

"You don't mean you ran into him," Mrs. Quinn said. "You mean you met him in the park."

"No, Mom. I mean I ran into him on my bike," Sean said. "But I didn't mean to. He kind of jumped into the way, but he didn't get hurt, so it's all right."

"I'm sorry I interrupted you," Mrs. Quinn said with a little sigh. "Tell us, what did Jacob say?"

"He said that while everyone in his family was at a family wedding in San Francisco, their house was burglarized."

"Oh, dear," Mrs. Quinn said.

"Yeah. The burglar took his parents' computer and fax machine and Jacob's video game. Jacob was really shaken up about someone going through their stuff and taking what they wanted."

"That's all they took? Electronics?" Brian asked.

Sean nodded. "That's it. I guess they got hit by the High-Tech Burglar."

"Did any of the neighbors see someone prowling around the house?"

"I asked Jacob, but he said no."

"There's something weird about those bur-glaries," Brian said. "How does the burglar know who has computers and stuff like that and who doesn't? And how does he know when the people are going to be out of the house?"

"Brian, suppose you stop asking questions and finish setting the table," Mrs. Quinn told him.

Brian went back to his job, but he said, "Mom, private investigators always start by asking questions. When they find the answers to their questions, they can usually solve the cases."

Sean pulled Brian to one side. "Are we on a case, Bri?" he asked eagerly. "Are we going to try to catch the High-Tech Burglar?"

Mr. Quinn scowled as he overheard Sean's question. "Absolutely not," he said. "Catching burglars is strictly up to the police."

"I've got one more question, Dad," Brian said. "How can the burglar get in and out of a house so fast, without being seen?"

"We've talked about this before," Mr. Quinn answered. "The average home burglary takes between five and seven minutes. If people have left their houses, the burglar can be pretty sure they won't be back within such a short time."

"But I mean *how*," Brian persisted.

"If doors don't have deadbolts, it can take only seconds to open them," Mr. Quinn said. "Burglars have the right tools, and they practice using them."

"Maybe Jacob's family told a lot of people they were going out of town to the wedding," Sean said.

"They might have," Mr. Quinn said. "The burglar may have picked up the information from overhearing people talking about the trip. Or sometimes thieves watch a house until they see a pattern. In any case, once burglars know a house is empty, they're in, they take what they want, and they're long gone by the time the house owners come home."

Sean and Brian looked at each other. They both felt a little uneasy thinking that some stranger might be secretly watching their family's comings and goings.

Brian quietly asked Sean, "Do you know where Jacob lives?"

"Sure," Sean said.

"Then let's ride over to his house after dinner. Mom and Dad couldn't answer all my questions about the burglary. Maybe Jacob can't either. But somewhere we're going to find the answers!"

5

THE DEANS' HOME was a comfortable, red brick house with a trim lawn and lots of shade trees. But there was nothing about it to make anyone think that the people who lived in it owned computers and color printers and fax machines and video games.

Brian pointed this out to Sean and added, "The Deans aren't super-rich."

"Hardly anybody we know is super-rich," Sean said. "But lots of them have either a VCR or a computer, and a lot of their kids have electronic games."

"Good point," Brian said. He made a nota-
tion in the small notebook he always had with
him.

Sean and Brian climbed the steps to the
Deans' porch and rang the bell.

Mrs. Dean, Jacob's mother, opened the door.

Brian introduced Sean and himself and
said, "We're trying to solve the case of the
High-Tech Burglar. Since we think he's the
one who burglarized you, would you mind
answering some questions for us?"

"Not at all," Mrs. Dean said. She sniffled into
a twisted handkerchief as she led Brian and
Sean to chairs in the living room. "Can you
imagine? Thieves prowling around inside our
house while we were spending the weekend in
San Francisco? I'll never forgive them for
invading our home and stealing things we
worked hard to buy."

"I understand they took only electronic equipment," Brian said.

"That's right," Mrs. Dean said. "And our computer was almost new!"

"Was it insured?" Brian asked.

"Why, no," Mrs. Dean said. "Only the partial amount that was covered under our homeowners policy. We didn't even think about getting extra insurance for it."

She began to dab at her nose again, so Sean changed the subject. "Did a lot of people know you were going to a family wedding?"

"Our neighbors did and the people at work—and the people at the travel agency, of course," Mrs. Dean answered. "They made travel arrangements for the bride and groom's honeymoon, too. And we told all our friends. Some of them gave a party for us at the Redoaks Yacht Club. There was even a little item about the party in last Wednesday's society section of the newspaper. Did you see it?"

"I guess I missed it," Sean said.

Mrs. Dean blew her nose and told Sean, "I'm sorry Jacob isn't here to play with you. He's at my brother's house."

"That's okay," Sean said. "Please just say hello to him for me."

They were almost at the door when Mrs. Dean stopped sniffling and took a close look at Brian. "Didn't you tell me that the two of you were trying to solve this case?" she asked.

"That's right," Brian said.

"But you're not old enough to be police officers."

"We're not police officers, Mrs. Dean," Brian replied. "We're private investigators. P.I.'s can be any age at all."

"Well, good luck," she said. But she stared

at Brian and Sean with a puzzled look in her eyes as they rode away on their bikes.

As soon as they turned the corner Sean said, "Bri, what if the burglar read in the newspaper about the party for the Deans at the Yacht Club, and that's how he knew they'd be away from home?"

"That could have happened," Brian answered. "Also, there may be someone who works at the restaurant in the Yacht Club who tips off the thief."

Sean sighed. "How are we going to figure out who it is?"

"Let's sleep on it," Brian said. "And tomorrow, see if you can think of any more questions to ask Jacob. I'm going to have to begin writing my news story. Both teams are meeting tomorrow afternoon at four, and filming starts after school."

Instead of getting to work on his news story when he arrived home, Brian said, "Mom, I have to ask you some questions."

"What kind of questions?" Mrs. Quinn asked.

"Questions about travel agents and how they arrange trips and honeymoons and stuff like that."

Mr. Quinn dropped his newspaper. "Honeymoons?"

"It's research, Dad. Mom, let's say if I wanted to get married—"

"If you *what*?" Mr. Quinn interrupted.

"Married," Brian said. "And if I told Mrs. Martinez I wanted her to plan a honeymoon, what would she do?"

"First of all, she'd ask if you knew where you wanted to travel, or if you'd like suggestions about interesting places. You might want a luxurious resort, or you might want a camping trip. And she'd ask you how much you'd want to spend on the trip."

"Would she keep it secret?"

"If you asked her to," Mrs. Quinn answered. "But there wouldn't be much reason to keep it secret, would there?"

Brian sighed. "I guess not."

Mr. Quinn studied Brian. "You're talking about honeymoons and keeping things secret? Brian, I think you and I should have a little talk."

Brian shook his head. "Not now, Dad. I've got a lot of things to think about."

Until bedtime Brian worked on the outline for his news report, listing the crime prevention ideas he wanted to include. He put in a call to the Quinn's family friend, Detective Sergeant Thomas Kerry, who agreed to be interviewed for the TV program.

Brian fell into bed, exhausted, his mind spinning with thoughts of break-in burglars, stolen computers, and Mrs. Martinez's travel agency. "Wait until tomorrow," he told himself, and then he fell asleep.

Mrs. Martinez's travel agency was open on Sunday afternoon, so Brian and Sean rode their bikes to the agency and went inside. Mrs. Martinez greeted them and introduced them to her assistant, Dana Garrett.

"I'd like to ask you some questions, Mrs. Martinez," Brian said.

Mrs. Martinez looked uncomfortable. She nervously twisted her fingers together as she asked, "Do these questions have anything to do with the *That's News 2 Me* television program?"

"Uh . . . yes and no," Brian answered.

Mrs. Martinez looked even more uncomfortable. "As you can see, both Miss Garrett and

I are busy with customers. I may not be able to get to you for a little while."

"That's all right," Brian said. "Sean and I won't mind waiting."

Brian picked up some travel brochures and handed a couple to Sean to read, but they were seated so close to Miss Garrett that they couldn't help overhearing her with her customer.

It was as if she were speaking to an old friend as she said, "Italy is lovely at that time of year, Mr. Banks. I'll give you some brochures to read, but you'll also find information about the country on the Internet. You do have access to the Internet, don't you?"

"Oh, yes," Mr. Banks answered.

"You can also get some wonderful pamphlets from the Italian Tourist Bureau. Here . . . I'll write down the addresses for you."

"Thank you," Mr. Banks said. "You provide

such wonderful services. I told my wife we wouldn't let anyone else handle our travel plans."

Miss Garrett smiled. "Be sure to turn on your household alarm system for extra protection."

Mr. Banks looked worried. "We've never put in an alarm system, I'm afraid."

"Don't give it a second thought," Miss Garrett said. "I don't have an alarm system either. It's just something we mention to all our customers."

Mr. Banks smiled and said, "I won't worry about a thing—except for having fun."

The elderly customer who followed Mr. Banks was just as happy with Miss Garrett's friendly approach.

"Miss Darvey, as I remember, you told me you had the cutest little West Highland terrier.

Would you like me to help you find a kennel that will board him while you're in Seattle for the week? Or will you have a pet sitter at your home?"

Miss Darvey smiled. "Dear Miss Garrett, you think of everything. You'll be happy to know I've already made plans to board Fritzi."

"I've insisted on a room with a bay view for you," Miss Garrett said, and she and Miss Darvey began to discuss the beauties of Seattle.

Finally, Mrs. Martinez left her customer and perched on the sofa next to Brian. In a low voice she asked, "Would you mind if I asked you to come back tomorrow, Brian? My customer's travel plans have become quite involved, and I won't be able to talk to you for at least another hour."

"That's okay, Mrs. Martinez," Brian said. "I'll come back."

As soon as Brian and Sean left the store, Sean said, "Miss Garrett seems to have more fun planning trips than Mrs. Martinez does. Mrs. Martinez seemed kinda quiet and even a little bit nervous every time she looked at you. Do you know why?"

Brian was surprised. "You noticed, too?"

"A good detective pays attention," Sean said and laughed as he poked Brian. "Isn't that what you always tell me?"

Brian smiled at Sean, and he said, "You're right. There *was* something bothering her, but I don't know what it was."

He didn't want to think of Estella's mother as a suspect in the high-tech burglaries. She couldn't be, Brian told himself. Or could she?

6

THE MEMBERS OF the two investigative teams got together at four o'clock at the Channel Two studios, all six of them on time.

"Take a look at this," Jack said, and held up a new video camera.

Holly gave it one glance and shouted, "Wow! That's expensive stuff. I couldn't afford a camera like that. I didn't think you could, either."

Jack turned red with embarrassment, and looked as though he wished he could hide his camera.

Brian knew that Jack's family was not well off, and for a moment he wondered, too, how Jack could afford equipment that cost so much. But he said, "That's a really great camera, Jack. It's perfect for a talented photographer like you."

Jack gave Brian a grateful smile. "Thanks," he said.

"Was your camera a birthday present?" Estella asked, and Jack's face turned red again.

"No," he mumbled. "I bought it for myself."

"Oh, sure," Holly teased. "How many banks did you have to rob to get the money for it?"

Jack glared at Holly. "It's none of—" he began, but Brian interrupted.

"Twenty-five," Brian said. "I helped him. C'mon, Holly. No more jokes. We've got a lot of work to do. Read my news story and tell me what you think."

As Holly read to herself, Brian thought about the camera and Jack's embarrassment and anger at Holly's blunt questions. Where *did* Jack come up with so much money? Could Jack be involved in the high-tech burglaries?

No! Brian told himself.

Holly shoved the pages of Brian's report at Mark. "This is okay," she said. "The part I like best is the interview with the detective. You're the photographer. See what you think about it."

As Estella's partners went over her script outline, Holly pointed out two changes Brian would need to make in his script. "Take out this site," she said. "It picks up too much traffic noise from the highway. Let's put it over on a quiet neighborhood street. And Mark and I agree that a playground background would be good when you talk about safety for younger kids. Okay?"

"Okay," Brian said. He was surprised that he liked the teamwork of sharing ideas. Mark's and Holly's ideas would make the whole story better.

Pete came in to take a look at what the teams had accomplished. He brought cans of soft drinks and a big bowl of popcorn and placed them on the table. For a few minutes no one thought of work.

Estella drew Brian aside, her eyes sparkling. "I've got some terrific news," she said.

"For *That's News 2 Me*?" Brian asked.

Estella giggled. "No. It's strictly my news, but I want to share it with you." She clasped her hands together and said, "Mom started a college savings plan for me years ago, but she couldn't afford to put much into it, so it's still pretty small. That's where my mom's Uncle Jake comes in. Mom told me he telephoned.

He said that he's adding a great deal of money to my college account—enough to take care of the whole four years!"

"That's super cool!" Brian said. "Uncle Jake must be a really great guy."

"Yes. He has to be."

Brian was surprised. "What do you mean, 'He has to be'? You make it sound like you never met him."

"I haven't," Estella answered. "It seems a little crazy, but Mom has never even mentioned him. She comes from a big family, but I've never heard of an Uncle Jake until now."

Brian was so startled he couldn't think of anything to say. He mumbled something about how everybody should have an Uncle Jake, but all he could think of was the large amount of money that was going to be put into Estella's college account. Where was it really coming from? Mrs. Martinez suddenly seemed like a very strong suspect in the case of the high-tech burglaries.

Estella rested a hand on Brian's arm, which made it tingle. "Mom said she was really nervous when you were at her travel agency. She was afraid you were there to talk her into being interviewed on television, and the idea of being on camera terrifies her. I hope you understand."

"Sure," Brian said, but he couldn't help wondering if this excuse was nothing more than Mrs. Martinez's attempt at a cover-up.

7

ON MONDAY afternoon Holly, Mark, and Brian met in front of the Quinn's house.

"This is where we open the story," Brian said. "I'll give just a few sentences about how we can watch for crime in our own neighborhoods. Okay?"

Mark studied the house and yard and looked through the viewfinder on his video camera. "Okay," he said. "Stand over there on the sidewalk. I'm going to shoot down the block, not just the one house."

Brian stood on the spot Mark indicated

while Holly adjusted her sound equipment. "Ready," Holly said.

Brian cleared his throat, tried not to think of all the people who'd be watching, and said into his hand mike, "Qyan Brinn here for *That's News 2 You*."

Holly doubled over laughing, and Mark yelled, "That's a wrap."

Brian had to laugh, too, but he felt a lot better when Mark said, "Lots of people get tongue-tied in front of a camera. There's no problem. We'll just start over."

Brian tried again. This time he said the opening line right, but Holly waved her hands and yelled, "Cut! The noise from that van is ruining everything."

Brian turned around to see a white van with an Appliance Repairs sign on the front door suddenly pull out of the Robinson's driveway, two houses away. Brian got a quick look at the driver of the van before it sped off.

"Take it again. Ready . . . start," Holly said, and they finished the shot.

"The next background is one street over," Holly said and grinned. "This time, just for fun, we'll be in front of *my* house."

Their equipment was light, so they carried it around the block. As they approached Holly's house she stopped. "Hey, wait a minute," she said. "There's another white van. What's it doing in our driveway?"

"Picking up your cleaning," Matt said. "Take a look at the sign on the side. It says, Speedy Dry Cleaning."

"It's not supposed to be there," Holly said. She put her sound equipment case on the lawn and ran toward her back door, Brian and Mark right behind her.

Suddenly, someone in a white uniform rushed out of the door, head down. He shoved Holly to the pavement and pushed Mark and Brian off their feet.

Even though he was lying in the bushes next to the driveway, Mark turned on his camera and filmed the man, who jumped into the van and backed it down the driveway.

Brian scrambled to his feet and ran after the van. As it bounced into the street he got a look at the driver. It was the same man he had seen in the *other* white van.

As Holly and Mark joined Brian, he wrote the license plate numbers on his script. "One van with an assortment of magnetic signs that can easily be changed," he said aloud. "No one would pay attention to it."

Holly bent to brush dirt off her jeans, and Brian said, "Are you all right? Did he hurt you?"

"I'm fine," Holly said. "What did that jerk think he was doing?"

"Burglarizing your house, I'm afraid," Brian answered. "Holly, let's look around inside and see if he got anything."

Brian and Mark followed Holly as she ran through the open kitchen door.

She pointed at a computer, printer, VCR, and fax machine that were piled on the floor, next to the door. "I bet he was going to carry those out to his van, only we surprised him," she said. Holly hugged her arms around her chest and began to shiver.

"It's okay, Holly," Mark said. "It's even better than okay because the burglar didn't get any of your stuff."

"But the creep was in our house," Holly complained. She shivered again.

"Is your mother at work? Call her," Brian

said, but Holly shook her head.

"Mom and Dad are on a business trip. Mom was worried enough about leaving me and my little brother with my aunt for a few days. I hate to call her about a burglary and scare her."

"Then call your aunt, and next call the police," Brian said. "No, don't call the police. I'll call myself and ask for Detective Kerry."

After Brian made his call he turned to Mark. "Did you take any pictures of the van?"

"Yes," Mark said, "but I made the first shots while I was lying on my back. The rest were made while I was running toward the street to keep the van in sight. I don't know how clear they're going to be."

Brian turned to Holly. "Did a travel agent arrange your parents' trip?"

Holly looked surprised. "Sure. Martinez Travel," she answered. "Miss Garrett arranges all my parents' trips—business and pleasure. But what has that got to do with anything?"

Brian got a lump in the pit of his stomach. Martinez Travel. One more clue that Estella's mother could be guilty.

Detective Kerry arrived within ten minutes and listened to Holly's story. He telephoned headquarters to put out information about the white van and its license plate numbers. Then he walked throughout the house with Holly as she looked for anything that might be missing.

"You kids have given us the best leads yet on this perp," Detective Kerry said.

"The High-Tech Burglar," Brian said.

Detective Kerry nodded, but he said, "I know you're working for a Channel Two news show, but I'm going to ask you to keep quiet about this. The High-Tech Burglar is targeting the Redoaks area, but he's selling the stolen items someplace else. As long as he thinks he won't get caught here, we have a chance of nabbing him."

Brian, Mark, and Holly agreed, and Mark handed Detective Kerry the film that had been in his camera. "It's okay if you keep this," he said. "We'll shoot again tomorrow and start from the beginning."

"We'll shoot that interview with you, too," Holly added.

Holly's aunt rushed into the house soon after Kerry had left. "I got your message!" she cried in a rush of words. "Jimmy and I were at the park! What did the burglar take? We'll call your parents."

"Everything's okay now, Aunt Marsha. Calm down," Holly said. She introduced Brian and Mark and told her aunt what had happened and how she'd gone all through the house with Detective Kerry.

"How did the burglar get in?" Marsha asked.

Holly looked surprised, but Brian had done the same kind of investigating that Detective Kerry had. They had both noted the scratches around the back-door lock.

Brian showed them to Marsha and Holly and pointed out, "You don't have deadbolts. Almost anyone could open a lock like this one."

"That settles it. We're having deadbolts installed today, if possible," Marsha insisted. "Here and at my house, too."

As Marsha drove Holly and Mark back to the television studio, Holly shouted out the car window, "Same place tomorrow afternoon at four-thirty!"

Brian walked toward home, but when he turned the corner he saw a police cruiser and a few neighbors in a cluster at the end of the Robinsons' driveway.

Sean suddenly broke from the group and ran to meet Brian.

"The Robinsons' house was hit by a burglar!" he yelled. "Mrs. Clooney was collecting the mail and watering the Robinsons' plants while they're on vacation, and she noticed that the back door was open!"

"What was taken?" Brian asked.

"Mrs. Clooney saw that their computer and printer and VCR were missing, but she doesn't know what else." Sean lowered his voice. "Do you think it was the High-Tech Burglar?"

"I think so," Brian said. He told Sean what had happened at Holly's house and added, "I'd better call Detective Kerry and tell him about the van I saw in the Robinsons' driveway."

Brian left a message, but it wasn't until nine o'clock that Kerry returned his call.

"We traced the van's license plates and a clear shot of the man's face that Mark got on film, and we came up with a positive I.D.," Detective Kerry said. "His name is Zeke Cunningham. He has a long record of burglaries, and he's now out of prison on probation. In the past he's operated out of San Francisco."

"Then that's where he's probably selling the stolen stuff," Brian said.

"That's what we think," Detective Kerry said.

"Does Zeke have any relatives or friends in Redoaks?" Brian asked.

"We're checking," Kerry answered. "But we haven't come up with anything. His only known relative is a sister named Barbara Cunningham. The address we have for her is in Ohio. We've asked the Cincinnati police to contact her."

"But Zeke must have some kind of connection here in Redoaks."

"Right," Kerry said. "Someone who knows which people are out of town and when they'll return."

Like Mrs. Martinez? Brian thought. He knew he should tell his suspicions to Detective Kerry, but he couldn't. If Brian were responsible for Mrs. Martinez being arrested, it would mean the end of his friendship with Estella.

Withholding information would be wrong, Brian knew. But he didn't have real, factual information. It was still only guesswork.

Brian gulped and said, "Thanks for your help, Detective Kerry. I hope you catch Zeke soon."

8

THE TELEPHONE rang as soon as Brian's call with Detective Kerry had ended. Brian was surprised to find it was Jack.

"I—uh—I've got to talk to you," Jack said. "Have you got a minute?"

"Sure," Brian said.

"It's . . . well, it's about my camera. I'm telling you, Brian, because you stood up for me when Holly . . ." He sighed and said, "I made a mistake getting so mad at Holly that I didn't . . . well, tell the truth."

Brian gripped the phone. "What are you talking about, Jack?"

"My camera," Jack said. "I shouldn't have brought it to the station, but I did because I was so proud of it."

"But you said you hadn't told the truth," Brian said. "What did you mean by that?"

"Oh. I told Holly I bought the camera myself, and I didn't. Just between you and me, Brian, my grandparents gave me the camera as a reward for staying out of trouble. I couldn't tell Holly that. I'd never hear the end of it."

Brian gave a huge sigh of relief. "It's okay, Jack," he said, and chuckled. "Holly doesn't have to know everything."

"Speaking of Holly, I heard that her house almost got robbed and you guys saw the robber," Jack said.

"How'd you hear that?" Brian asked. "We were supposed to keep quiet about it."

"She didn't tell me it was a secret," Jack said.

"She? Who's *she*? Holly?"

"No, Estella," Jack said. "But Holly may have told her."

"Yeah," Brian said. That lump was coming back in his stomach. He managed to say good-bye to Jack, then leaned against the wall, trying to think. It might not have been Holly who told Estella. It might have been . . . to Brian's surprise, the facts were beginning to add up to another possible answer.

Sean stopped in front of Brian. "What's the matter with you, Bri? You look weird."

"We've got to talk," Brian told him. "I learned a couple of things tonight that you should know, too. The Casebusters have got to get busy."

Brian told Sean about the phone conversations with Detective Kerry and with Jack.

Then he took a deep breath and said, "I don't have to film until four-thirty, so right after school you and I are going to the Martinez Travel Agency. There's one very important question we have to ask."

Sean looked puzzled. "Ask who?"

"I've got to think about it some more," Brian answered. "Okay?"

"Sure, okay," Sean said. He studied Brian. "It has to do with Estella, doesn't it?"

"I told you," Brian said, "that I've got to do some more thinking." He felt a cold chill run up and down his backbone as he wondered if he was right and if his idea would really work.

*   *   *

The next afternoon Brian and Sean set off on their bikes for town.

"C'mon this way," Brian said. "Let's take

the side streets. We'll get to the travel agency faster than if we have to deal with the traffic on the boulevard."

"Are you sure this will work?" Sean asked.

"All we can do is try," Brian said.

"Bri," Sean said.

"I mean, a lot depends on the answer, but—"

"Bri," Sean tried again.

"If she—"

"Listen to me!" Sean interrupted. "There's a white van back there. It turned off when we did. I think he's following us."

"White van?" Brian turned around, trying to catch a look at the driver.

The van speeded up, heading straight for Brian and Sean.

"Help!" Sean yelled, but no one was around to hear or see what was happening.

"He's going to run us down!" Sean shouted.

"On the sidewalk! Quick!" Brian yelled.

He and Sean jumped the curb and cut across the yard of the house on the corner. They heard the smack of tires as the van leaped the curb and came after them.

"The trees!" Brian called to Sean. "Make for the trees!"

As they shot between two trees they heard the screech of the van's brakes. Its wheels ground up chunks of lawn and mud as it backed up.

A woman ran out of the house, screaming at the driver of the van. Someone in a big station wagon drove up and honked at him. A couple of neighbors appeared.

The van bounced onto the street, did a U-turn, and sped away.

"Are you boys all right?" the woman called

to Brian and Sean. "He could have killed you!"

"We're okay, thanks," Brian said.

"But awfully scared," Sean whispered.

"I got his license number," the woman said, "and the name of the house painting company on the side of his van. I'll call the police."

The driver of the station wagon held up a cellular phone. "I already called them."

A police car arrived within a few minutes, and Brian and Sean told the officer that the van had sped up, heading for them, and they had escaped by riding through a cluster of trees.

The neighbors verified the story and added information of their own. After writing down names and addresses and taking some photos of the torn-up lawn, the police officer left.

"Should we go home?" Sean asked Brian as they headed down the street.

"No," Brian said. "The High-Tech Burglar

will try to stay out of sight to avoid the police who'll come looking for him. What we need to do most is catch him. That's why we have to visit the travel agency."

As they entered the agency Brian and Sean could see that both Mrs. Martinez and Miss Garrett were busy with customers. Mrs. Martinez looked up and gave them a smile, but Miss Garrett was giggling with her customer about something funny that had happened in a restaurant in Mexico City.

Brian and Sean began looking through a stack of travel brochures near Miss Garrett's desk. But gradually and quietly, Brian began moving behind the desk. Suddenly he said loudly, "Barbara Cunningham?"

Miss Garrett half turned and answered, "Yes?"

Her mouth dropped open. She managed to

pull herself together and said, "I'm not—"

"Yes, you are," Brian told her. "You're Zeke Cunningham's sister. You've been helping him to steal from empty homes in Redoaks by letting him know who is going out of town and how long they'll be away from home."

"What?" Mrs. Martinez dropped her pencil and stood up.

Miss Garrett's customer gave a little shriek. "That can't be true!" she said. "Dana's the most helpful, most friendly travel agent I've ever met."

"Is it friendliness or nosiness?" Brian asked. "I've heard Miss Garrett with her customers. She finds out all sorts of things, like if they have an alarm system, if they own a dog, and if it will be boarded. She gets all the information she needs to pass on to her brother, Zeke Cunningham."

Brian motioned to Sean. "Use one of those

phones over there to call Detective Kerry."

"Now, wait a minute," Miss Garrett said. She tried to rise, but Mrs. Martinez stepped up behind her and firmly pushed her back into her chair.

"Please stay here until the police come, Dana," Mrs. Martinez said.

Miss Cunningham squirmed, trying to break loose from Mrs. Martinez's grip. "Are you going to pay any attention to these boys?" Miss Cunningham complained. "They're nothing but a couple of kids."

"Correction," Sean said. "We're a couple of kids who help our dad and the police solve crimes. We're the Casebusters."

"And TV reporters, too," Brian added. He thought about Estella and how happy she'd be with his story. He couldn't help grinning with relief.

"As soon as Detective Kerry gets here, I'll call the news desk at Channel Two," Brian said. "There's plenty of time for the story about the capture of the High-Tech Burglars to make the evening news."

JOAN LOWERY NIXON is a renowned writer of children's mysteries. She is the author of more than eighty books and the only four-time recipient of the prestigious Edgar Allan Poe Award for the best juvenile mystery of the year.

☾

"I was asked by Disney Adventures *magazine if I could write a short mystery. I decided to write about two young boys who help their father, a private investigator, solve crimes. These boys, Brian and Sean, are actually based on my grandchildren, who are the same ages as the characters. My first Casebusters story was a piece about a ghost that haunts an inn. This derives from a legendary Louisiana inn I visited, which was allegedly haunted. Later, I learned the owner had made up the entire tale, and I used that angle in the story."* — JOAN LOWERY NIXON